I0819746

CONTAMINATION CREW

Start Publishing PD LLC

Manufactured in the United States of America

Cover art: Shutterstock/Taisiya Kozorez

Cover design: Jennifer Do

10 9 8 7 6 5 4 3 2 1

ISBN 979-8-8809-0343-6

CONTAMINATION CREW

by Alan E. Nourse

(The following is taken from the files of the Medical Disciplinary Board, Hospital Earth, from the preliminary hearings in re: The Profession vs. Samuel B. Jenkins, Physician; First Court of Medical Affairs, final action pending.)

COM COD S221VB73 VOROCHISLOV SECTOR; 4th GALACTIC PERIOD 22, 2341 GENERAL SURVEY SHIP *MERCY* TO HOSPITAL EARTH

VIA: FASTEST POSSIBLE ROUTING, PRIORITY UNASSIGNED

TO: Lucius Darby,

Physician Grade I, Black Service Director of Galactic
Periphery Services, Hospital Earth

FROM: Samuel B. Jenkins, Physician Grade VI, Red Service General
Practice Patrol Ship *Lancet* (Attached GSS *Mercy* pro tem)

SIR: The following communication is directed to your attention in hopes that it may anticipate various charges which are certain to be placed against me as a Physician of the Red Service upon the return of the General Survey Ship *Mercy* to Hospital Earth (expected arrival four months from above date).

These charges will undoubtedly be preferred by one Turvold Neelsen, Physician Grade II of the Black Service, and Commander of the *Mercy* on its current survey mission into the Vorochislov Sector. Exactly what the charges will be I cannot say, since the Black Doctor in question refuses either audience or communication with me at the present time; however, it seems likely that treason, incompetence and mutinous insubordination will be among the milder complaints registered. It is possible that even Malpractice might be added, so you can readily understand the reasons for this statement—

CONTAMINATION CREW

The following will also clarify my attached request that the GSS *Mercy*, upon arrival in orbit around Hospital Earth, be met immediately by a decontamination ship carrying a vat of hydrochloric acid, concentration 3.7%, measuring no less than twenty by thirty by fifty feet, and that Quarantine officials be prepared to place the entire crew of the *Mercy* under physical and psychiatric observation for a period of no less than six weeks upon disembarkation.

The facts, in brief, are as follows:

Three months ago, as crew of the General Practice Patrol Ship *Lancet*, my colleague Green Doctor Wallace Stone and myself began investigating certain peculiar conditions existing on the fourth planet of Mauki, Vorochislov Sector (Class I Medical Service Contract.) The entire population of that planet was found to be suffering from a mass psychotic delusion of rather spectacular proportions: namely, that they and their entire planet were in imminent danger of being devoured, in toto, by an indestructible non-humanoid creature which they called a *hlorg*. The Maukivi were insistent that a *hlorg* had already totally consumed a non-existent outer planet in their system, and was now hard at work on neighboring Mauki V. It was their morbid fear that Mauki IV was next on its list. No amount of reassurance could convince them of the foolishness of these fears, although we exhausted our energy, our patience, and our food and medical supplies in the effort. Ultimately we referred the matter to the Grey Service, feeling confident that it was a psychiatric problem rather than medical or surgical. We applied to the GSS *Mercy* to take us aboard to replenish our ship's supplies, and provide us a much-needed recovery period. The Black Doctor in command approved our request and brought us aboard.

The trouble began two days later....

*

There were three classes of dirty words in use by the men who travelled the spaceways back and forth from Hospital Earth.

There were the words you seldom used in public, but which were colorful and descriptive in private use.

Then there were the words which you seldom used even in private, but which effectively relieved feelings when directed at mirrors, inanimate objects, and people who had just left the room.

Finally, there were the words that you just didn't use, period. You knew they existed; you'd heard them used at one time or another, but to hear them spoken out in plain Earth-English was enough to rock the most space-hardened of the Galactic Pill Peddlers back on his well-worn heels.

Black Doctor Turvold Neelsen's Earth-English was spotty at best, but the word came through without any possibility of misinterpretation. Red Doctor Sam Jenkins stared at the little man and felt his face turning as scarlet as the lining of his uniform cape.

"But that's ridiculous!" he finally stammered. "Quite aside from the language you use to suggest it."

"Ah! So the word still has some punch left, eh? At least you puppies bring something away from your Medical Training, even if it's only taboos." The Black Doctor scowled across the desk at Jenkins' lanky figure. "But sometimes, my good Doctor, it is better to face a fact than to wait for the fact to face you. Sometimes we have to crawl out of our ivory towers for a minute or two—you know?"

Jenkins reddened again. He had never had any great love for physicians of the Black Service—who did?—but he found himself disliking this short, blunt-spoken man even more cordially than most. "Why implicate the *Lancet*?" he burst out. "You've landed the *Mercy* on plenty of planets before we brought the *Lancet* aboard her—"

"But we did not have it with us before the *Lancet* came aboard, and we do have it now. The implication is obvious. You have brought aboard a contaminant."

He'd said it again.

Red Doctor Jenkins' face darkened. "The Green Doctor and I have maintained the *Lancet* in perfect conformity with the Sterility Code.

We've taken every precaution on both landing and disembarking procedures. What's more, we've spent the last three months on a planet with *no* mutually compatible flora or fauna. From Hospital Earth viewpoint, Mauki IV is sterile. We made only the briefest check-stop on Mauki V before joining you. It was a barren rock, but we decontaminated again after leaving. If you have a—a *contaminant* on board your ship, sir, it didn't come from the *Lancet*. And I won't be held responsible."

It was strong language to use to a Black Doctor, and Sam Jenkins knew it. There were doctors of the Green and Red Services who had spent their professional lives on some god-forsaken planetoid at the edge of the Galaxy for saying less. Red Doctor Sam Jenkins was too near the end of his Internship, too nearly ready for his first Permanent Planetary Appointment with the rank, honor, and responsibility it carried to lightly risk throwing it to the wind at this stage—

But a Red Doctor does not bring a contaminant aboard a survey ship, he thought doggedly, no matter what the Black Doctor says—

Neelsen looked at the young man slowly. Then he shrugged. "Of course, I'm merely a pathologist. I realize that we know nothing of medicine, nor of disease, nor of the manner in which disease is spread. All this is beyond our scope. But perhaps you'll permit one simple question from a dull old man, just to humor him."

Jenkins looked at the floor. "I'm sorry, sir."

"Just so. You've had a very successful cruise this year with the *Lancet*, I understand."

Jenkins nodded.

"A most successful cruise. Four planets elevated from Class IV to Class II contracts, they tell me. Morua II elevated from Class VI to Class I, with certain special riders. A plague-panic averted on Setman I, and a very complex virus-bacteria symbiosis unravelled on Orb III. An illustrious record. You and your colleague from the Green Service are hoping for a year's exemption from training, I imagine—" The

Black Doctor looked up sharply. "You searched your holds after leaving the Mauki planets, I presume?"

Jenkins blinked. "Why—no, sir. That is, we decontaminated according to—"

"I see. You didn't search your holds. I suppose you didn't notice your food supplies dwindling at an alarming rate?"

"No—" The Red Doctor hesitated. "Not really."

"Ah." The Black Doctor closed his eyes wearily and flipped an activator switch. The scanner on the far wall buzzed into activity. It focussed on the rear storage hold of the *Mercy* where the little *Lancet* was resting on its landing rack. "Look closely, Doctor."

At first Jenkins saw nothing. Then his eye caught a long, pink glistening strand lying across the floor of the hold. The scanner picked up the strand, followed it to the place where it emerged from a neat pencil-sized hole in the hull of the *Lancet*. The strand snaked completely across the room and disappeared through another neat hole in the wall into the next storage hold.

Jenkins shook his head as the scanner flipped back to the hole in the *Lancet*'s hull. Even as he watched, the hole enlarged and a pink blob began to emerge. The blob kept coming and coming until it rested soggily on the edge of the hole. Then it teetered and fell *splat* on the floor.

"Friend of yours?" the Black Doctor asked casually.

It was a pink heap of jelly just big enough to fill a scrub bucket. It sat on the floor, quivering noxiously. Then it sent out pseudopods in several directions, probing the metal floor. After a few moments it began oozing along the strand of itself that lay on the floor, and squeezed through the hole into the next hold.

"Ugh," said Sam Jenkins, feeling suddenly sick.

"The hydroponic tanks are in there," the Black Doctor said. "You've seen one of those before?"

"Not in person." Jenkins shook his head weakly. "Only pictures. It's a *hlorg*. We thought it was only a Maukivi persecution fantasy."

"This thing is growing pretty fast for a persecution fantasy. We spotted it eight hours ago, demolishing what was left of your food supply. It's twice as big now as it was then."

"Well, we've got to get rid of it," said Jenkins, suddenly coming to life.

"Amen, Doctor."

"I'll get the survey crew alerted right away. We won't waste a minute. And my apologies." Jenkins was hurrying for the door. "I'll get it cleared out of here fast."

"I do hope so," said the Black Doctor. "The thing makes me ill just to think about."

"I'll give you a clean-ship report in twenty-four hours," the Red Doctor said as confidently as he could and beat a hasty retreat down the corridor. He was wishing fervently that he felt as confident as he sounded.

The Maukivi had described the *hlorg* in excruciating detail. He and Green Doctor Stone had listened, and smiled sadly at each other, day after day, marvelling at the fanciful delusion. *Hlorgs*, indeed! And such creatures to dream up—eating, growing, devouring plant, animal and mineral without discrimination—

And the Maukivi had stoutly maintained that this *hlorg* of theirs was indestructible—

*

Green Doctor Wally Stone, true to his surgical calling, was a man of action.

"You mean there *is* such a thing?" he exploded when his partner confronted him with the news. "For real? Not just somebody's pipe dream?"

"There is," said Jenkins, "and we've got it. Here. On board the *Mercy*. It's eating like hell-and-gone and doubling its size every eight hours."

"Well what are you waiting for? Toss it overboard!"

"Fine! And what happens to the next party it happens to land on? We're supposed to be altruists, remember? We're supposed to worry about the health of the Galaxy." Jenkins shook his head. "Whatever we do with it, we have to find out just what we're tossing before we toss."

The creature had made itself at home aboard the *Mercy*. In the spirit of uninvited guests since time immemorial, it had established a toehold with remarkable asperity, and now was digging in for the long winter. Drawn to the hydroponic tanks like a flea to a dog, the *hlorg* had settled its bulbous pink body down in their murky depths with a contented gurgle. As it grew larger the tank-levels grew lower, the broth clearer.

The fact that the twenty-five crewmen of the *Mercy* depended on those tanks for their food supply on the four-month run back to Hospital Earth didn't seem to bother the *hlorg* a bit. It just sank down wetly and began to eat.

Under Jenkins' whip hand, and with Green Doctor Stone's assistance, the Survey Crew snapped into action. Survey was the soul and lifeblood of the medical services supplied by Hospital Earth to the inhabited planets of the Galaxy. Centuries before, during the era of exploration, every Earth ship had carried a rudimentary Survey Crew—a physiologist, a biochemist, an immunologist, a physician—to determine the safety of landings on unknown planets. Other races were more advanced in technological and physical sciences, in sales or in merchandising—but in the biological sciences men of Earth stood unexcelled in the Galaxy. It was not surprising that their casual offerings of medical services wherever their ships touched had led to a growing demand for those services, until the first Medical Service Contract with Deneb III had formalized the planetary specialty. Earth had become Hospital Earth, physician to a Galaxy, surgeon to a thousand worlds, midwife to those susceptible to midwifery and psychiatrist to those whose inner lives zigged when their outer lives zagged.

In the early days it had been a haphazard arrangement; but gradually distinct Services appeared to handle problems of medicine, surgery, radiology, psychiatry and all the other functions of a well-appointed medical service. Under the direction of the Black Service of Pathology, Hospital ships and Survey ships were dispatched to serve as bases for the tiny General Practice Patrol ships that answered the calls of the planets under Contract.

But it was the Survey ships that did the basic dirty-work on any new planet taken under Contract—outlining the physiological and biochemical aspects of the races involved, studying their disease patterns, their immunological types, their susceptibility to medical, surgical, or psychiatric treatment. It was an exacting service to perform, and Survey did an exacting job.

Now, with their own home base invaded by a hungry pink jelly-blob, the Survey Crew of the *Mercy* dug in with all fours to find a way to exorcise it.

The early returns were not encouraging.

Bowman, the anatomist, spent six hours with the creature. He'd go after the functional anatomy first, he thought, as he approached the task with gusto. Special organs, vital organ systems—after all, every Achilles had his heel. Functional would spot it if anything would—

Six hours later he rendered a preliminary report. It consisted of a blank sheet of paper and an expression of wild frustration.

"What's this supposed to mean?" Jenkins asked.

"Just what it says."

"But it says nothing!"

"That's exactly what it means." Bowman was a thin, wistful-looking man with a hawk nose and a little brown mustache. He subbed as ship's cook when things were slow in his specialty. He wasn't a very good cook, but what could anyone do with the sludge from the harvest shelf of a hydroponic tank? Now, with the *hlorg* incumbent, there wasn't even any sludge.

"I drained off a tank and got a good look at it before it crawled over into the next one," Bowman said. "Ugly bastard. But from a strictly anatomical standpoint I can't help you a bit."

Green Doctor Stone glowered over Jenkins' shoulder at the man. "But surely you can give us *something.*"

Bowman shrugged. "You want it technical?"

"Any way you like."

"Your *hlorg* is an ideal anamorph. A nothing. Protoplasm, just protoplasm."

Jenkins looked up sharply. "What about his cellular organization?"

"No cells," said Bowman. "Unless they're sub-microscopic, and I'd need an electron-peeker to tell you that."

"No organ systems?"

"Not even an integument. You saw how slippery he looked? That's why. There's nothing holding him in but energy."

"Now, look," said Stone. "He eats, doesn't he? He must have waste materials of some sort."

Bowman shook his head unhappily. "Sorry. No urates. No nitrates. No CO_2. Anyway, he doesn't eat because he has nothing to eat with. He absorbs. And that includes the lining of the tanks, which he seems to like as much as the contents. He doesn't *bore* those holes he makes—he *dissolves* them."

They sent Bowman back to quarters for a hot bath and a shot of Happy-O and looked up Hrunta, the biochemist.

Hrunta was glaring at paper electrophoretic patterns and pulling out chunks of hair around his bald spot. He gave them a snarl and shoved a sheaf of papers into their hands.

"Metabolic survey?" Jenkins asked.

"Plus," said Hrunta. "You're not going to like it, either."

"Why not? If it grows, it metabolizes. If it metabolizes, we can kill it. Axiom number seventeen, paragraph number four."

"Oh, it metabolizes, all right, but you'd better find yourself another axiom, pretty quick."

"Why?"

"Because it not only metabolizes, it *consumes*. There's no sign of the usual protein-carbohydrate-fat metabolism going on here. This baby has an enzyme system that's straight from hell. It bypasses the usual metabolic activities that produce heat and energy and gets right down to basic-basic."

Jenkins swallowed. "What do you mean?"

"It attacks the nuclear structure of whatever matter the creature comes in contact with. There's a partial mass-energy conversion in its rawest form. The creature goes after carbon-bearing substances first, since the C seems to break down more easily than anything else—hence its preference for plant and animal material over non-C stuff. But it can use anything if it has to—"

Jenkins stared at the little biochemist, an image in his mind of the pink creature in the hold, growing larger by the minute as it ate its way through the hydroponics, through the dry stores, through—

"Is there anything it *can't* use?"

"If there is, I haven't found it," Hrunta said sadly. "In fact, I can't see any reason why it couldn't consume this ship and everything in it, right down to the last rivet—"

*

They walked down to the hold for another look at their uninvited guest, and almost wished they hadn't.

It had reached the size of a small hippopotamus, although the resemblance ended there. Twenty hours had elapsed since the survey had begun. The *hlorg* had used every minute of it, draining the tanks, engulfing dry stores, devouring walls and floors as it spread out in search of food, leaving trails of eroded metal wherever it went.

It was ugly—ugly in its pink shapelessness, ugly in its slimy half-sentient movements, in its very *purposefulness*. But its ugliness went even deeper, stirring primordial feelings of revulsion and loathing in their minds as they watched it oozing implacably across the hold to another dry-storage bin.

Wally Stone shuddered. "It's *grown.*"

"Too fast. Bowman charts it as geometric progression."

Stone scratched his jaw as a lone pink pseudopod pushed out on the floor toward him. Then he leaped forward and stamped on it, severing the strand from the body.

The severed member quivered and lay still for a moment. Then it flowed back to rejoin the body with a wet gurgle.

Stone looked at his half-dissolved shoe.

"Egotropism," Jenkins said. "Bowman played around with that, too. A severed piece will rejoin if it can. If it can't it just takes up independent residence and we have two *hlorgs.*"

"What happens to it outside the ship?" Stone wanted to know.

"It falls dormant for several hours, and then splits up into a thousand independent chunks. One of the boys spent half of yesterday out there gathering them up. I tell you, this thing is equipped to *survive.*"

"So are we," said Green Doctor Stone grimly. "If we can't outwit this free-flowing gob of obscenity, we deserve anything we get. Let's have a conference."

They met in the pilot room. The Black Doctor was there; so were Bowman and Hrunta. Chambers, the physiologist, was glumly clasping and unclasping his hands in a corner. The geneticist, Piccione, drew symbols on a scratch pad and stared blankly at the wall.

Jenkins was saying: "Of course, these are only preliminary reports, but they serve to outline the problem. This is not just an annoyance any longer, it's a crisis. We'd all better understand that."

The Black Doctor cut him off with a wave of his hand, and glowered at the papers as he read them through minutely. As he sat hunched at the desk with the black cowl of his office hanging down from his shoulders he looked like a squat black judge, Jenkins thought, a shadow from the Inquisition, a Passer of Spells. But there was no medievalism in Black Doctor Neelsen. In fact, it was for that reason, and only that reason, that the Black Service had come to be the leaders and the whips, the executors and directors of all the manifold operations of Hospital Earth.

*

The physicians of the General Practice Patrol were fledglings, newly trained in their specialties, inexperienced in the rigorous discipline of medicine that was required of the directors of permanent Planetary Dispensaries in the heavily populated systems of the Galaxy. On outlying worlds where little was known of the ways of medicine, the temptation was great to substitute faith for knowledge, cant for investigation, nonsense rituals for hard work. But the physicians of the Black Service were always waiting to jerk wandering neophytes back to the scientific disciplines that made the service of Hospital Earth so effective. The Black Doctors would not tolerate sloppiness. "Show me the tissue, Doctor," they would say. "Prove to me that what you say is so. Prove that what you did was valid medicine...." Their laboratories were the morgues and autopsy rooms of a thousand planets, the Temples of Truth from which no physician since the days of Pasteur and Lister could escape for long and retain his position.

The Black Doctors were the pragmatists, the gadflies of Hospital Earth.

For this reason it was surprising to hear Black Doctor Neelsen saying, "Perhaps we are being too scientific, just now. When the creature has exhausted our food stores, it will look elsewhere for food. Perhaps we must cut at the tree and not at the root."

"A frontal attack?" said Jenkins.

"Just so. Its enzyme system is its vulnerability. Enzyme systems operate under specific optimum conditions, right? And every known enzyme system can be inactivated by adverse conditions of one sort or another. A physical approach may tell us how in this case. Meanwhile we will be on emergency rations, and hope that we don't starve to death finding out." The Black Doctor paused, looking at the men around him. "And in case you are thinking of enlisting help from outside, forget it. I've sent plague-warnings out for Galactic relay. We have this thing isolated, and we're going to keep it that way as long as I command this ship."

They went gloomily back to their laboratories to plan their frontal attack.

That was the night that Hrunta disappeared.

*

He was gone when they came to wake him from his sleep period. His bunk had been slept in, but he wasn't in it. In fact, he wasn't anywhere on the ship.

"But he couldn't just vanish!" the Black Doctor burst out when they told him the news. "Maybe he's hiding somewhere. Maybe this business was working on his mind."

Green Doctor Stone took a crew of men to search the ship again, even though he considered it a waste of precious time. He had his private convictions about where Hrunta had gone.

So did every other man on the ship, including Jenkins.

The *hlorg* had stopped eating. Huge and round and wet and ugly, it squatted in the after-hold, quivering gently, without any other sign of life.

Surfeited. Like a fat man after a turkey dinner.

Jenkins reviewed progress with the others. No stone had been left unturned. They had sliced the *hlorg*, and squeezed it. They had boiled it and frozen it. They had dropped chunks of it in acid vats and covered other chunks with desiccants and alkalis. Nothing seemed to bother it.

A cold environment slowed down its activity, true, but it also stimulated the process of fission. Warmed up again, the portions sucked back together again and resumed eating.

Heat was a little more effective, but not much. It stunned the creature for a brief period, but it would not burn. It hissed frightfully and gave off an overpowering stench, and curled up at the edges, but as soon as the heat was turned off it began to recover.

In Hrunta's lab chunks of the *hlorg* sat in a dozen vats on tables and in sinks. Some contained antibiotics, some concentrated acids, some desiccants. In each vat a blob of pink protoplasm wiggled happily, showing no sign of discomfiture. On another table were the remains of Hrunta's (unsuccessful) attempt to prepare an anti-*hlorg* serum.

But no Hrunta.

"He was down there with the thing all day," Bowman said sadly. "He felt it was his responsibility, really. Hrunta thought biochemistry was the answer to all things, of course. Very conscientious man."

"But he was in *bed*."

"He claimed he did his best thinking in bed. Maybe he had a brainstorm and went down to try it out, and—"

"Yes." Jenkins nodded sourly. "And." He walked down the row of vats. "You'd think that at least concentrated sulphuric would dessicate it a little. But it's just formed a crust of coagulated protein around itself, and sits there—"

Bowman peered over his shoulder, his mustache twitching. "But it does dessicate."

"If you use enough long enough."

"How about concentrated hydrochloric?"

"Same thing. Maybe a little more effective, but not enough to count."

"Okay. Next we try combinations. There's got to be *something* the wretched beast can't tolerate—"

There was, of course.

*

Green Doctor Stone brought it to Jenkins as he was getting ready to turn in for a sleep period. Jenkins had checked to make sure double guards were posted in the *hlorg's* vicinity, and jolted them with Sleep-Not to keep them on their toes. All the same, he tied a length of stout cord around his ankle just to make sure he didn't do any sleepwalking. He was tying it to the bunk when Stone came in with a pan in his hand and a peculiar look on his face.

"Take a look at this," he said.

Jenkins looked at the sickly brown mass in the tray, and then up at Stone. "Where did you find it?"

"Down in the hold. Our *hlorg* has broken precedent. It's *rejected* something that it ate."

"Yeah. What is it?"

"I don't know. I'm taking it to Neelsen for paraffin sections. But I know what it looks like to me."

"Mm. I know." Jenkins felt sick. Stone headed up to the path lab, leaving the Red Doctor settled in his bunk.

Ten minutes later Jenkins sat bolt upright in the darkness. Frantically he untied himself and slid into his clothes. "Idiot!" he growled to himself. "Seventh son of a seventh son—"

Five minutes later he was staring at the vats in Hrunta's laboratory. He found the one he was looking for. A pink blob of *hlorg* wiggled slowly around the bottom.

Jenkins drew a beaker of distilled water and added it to the fluid in the vat. It hissed and sputtered and sent up quantities of acrid steam. When the steam had cleared away, Jenkins peered in eagerly.

The pink thing in the bottom was turning a sickly violet. It had quit wiggling. As Jenkins watched, the violet color changed to mud grey, then to black. He prodded it with a stirring rod. There was no response.

With a whoop Jenkins buzzed Bowman and Stone. "We've got it!" he shouted to them when they appeared. "Look! Look at it!"

Bowman poked and probed and broke into a wide grin. The piece of *hlorg* was truly and sincerely dead. "It inactivates the enzyme system, and renders the base protoplasm vulnerable to anything that normally attacks it. What are we waiting for?"

They began tearing the laboratory apart, searching for the right bottles. The supply was discouragingly small, but there was some in stock. The three of them raced down the corridor for the hold where the *hlorg* was.

It took them three hours of angry work to exhaust the supply. They whittled chunks off the *hlorg*, tossed them in pans of the deadly fluid. With each slice they stopped momentarily to watch it turn violet, then black, as it died. The *hlorg*, dwindling in size, sensed the attack and slapped frantically at their ankles, sending out angry plumes of wet jelly, but they ducked and dodged and whittled some more. The *hlorg* quivered and gurgled and wept pinkish goo all over the floor, but it grew smaller and weaker with every whack.

"Hrunta must have spotted it and come down here alone," Jenkins panted between slices. "Maybe he slipped, lost his footing, I don't know—"

They continued to work until the supply was exhausted. They had reduced the *hlorg* to a quarter its previous size. "Check the other labs, see if they have some more," said Stone.

"I already have," Bowman said. "They don't. This is it."

"But we haven't got it all killed. There's still—" He pointed to the thing quailing in the corner.

"I know. We're licked, that's all. There isn't any more of the stuff on the ship."

They stopped and looked at each other suddenly. Then Jenkins said: "Oh, yes there is."

There was silence. Bowman looked at Stone, and Stone looked at Bowman. They both looked at Jenkins. "Oh, no. Sorry. I decline." Stone shook his head slowly.

"But we have to! There's no other way. If the enzyme system is inactivated, it's just protoplasm—there's no physiological or biochemical reason—"

"You know what you can do with your physiology and biochemistry," Bowman said succinctly. "You can also count me out." He left them and the hatchway clanged after him.

"Wally?"

"Yeah."

"It'll be months before we get back to Hospital Earth. We know how we can hold it in check until we get there."

"Yeah."

"Well?"

Green Doctor Wally Stone sighed. "Greater love hath no man," he said wearily. "We'd better go tell Neelsen, I guess."

*

Black Doctor Turvold Neelsen's answer was a flat, unequivocal no. "It's monstrous and preposterous. I won't stand for it. Nobody will stand for it."

"But you have the proof in your own hands," Jenkins said. "You saw the specimen that the Green Doctor brought you."

Neelsen hunched back angrily. "I saw it."

"And your impression of it? As a pathologist?"

"I fail to see how my impression applies one way or the other—"

"Doctor, sometimes we have to face facts. Remember?"

"All right." Neelsen seemed to curl up into himself still further. "The specimen was stomach."

"Human stomach?"

"Human stomach."

"But the only human on this ship that doesn't have a stomach is Hrunta," said Jenkins.

"So the *hlorg* ate him."

"*Most* of him. Not quite all. It threw out the one part of him it couldn't eat. The part containing a substance that inactivated its enzyme system. Dilute hydrochloric acid, to be specific. We used the entire ship's supply, and cut the *hlorg* down to three-quarters size, but we need a continuous supply to keep it whittled down until we get home. And there's only one good, permanent, reliable source of dilute hydrochloric acid on board this ship—"

The Black Doctor's face was purple. "I said no," he choked. "My answer stands."

The Red Doctor sighed and turned to Green Doctor Stone. "All right, Wally," he said.

*

(From the files of the Medical Disciplinary Board, Hospital Earth, op. cit.)

I am certain that you can see from the foregoing that a reasonable effort was made by Green Doctor Stone and myself to put the plan in effect peaceably and with full approval of our commander. It was our conviction, however, that the emergency nature of the circumstances required that it be done with or without his approval. Our subsequent success in containing the *hlorg* to at least reasonable and manageable proportions should bear out the wisdom of our decision.

Actually, it has not been as bad as one might think. It has been necessary to confine the crew to their quarters, and to restrain the Black Doctor forcibly, but with liberal use of Happy-O we can occasionally convince ourselves that it is rare beefsteak, and the Green Doctor, our pro-tem cook has concocted several very tasty sauces, such as mushroom, onion, etc. We reduce the *hlorg* to half its size each day, and if thoroughly heated the chunks lie still on the plate for quite some time.

No physical ill effects have been noted, and the period of quarantine is recommended solely to allow the men an adequate period for psychological recovery.

I have only one further recommendation: that the work team from the Grey Service be recalled at once from their assignment on Mauki IV. The problem is decidedly not psychiatric, and it would be one of the tragedies of the ages if our excellent psychiatric service were to succeed in persuading the Maukivi out of their 'delusion'.

After all, Hospital Earth cannot afford to jeopardize a Contract—

(Signed) Samuel B. Jenkins,
Physician Grade VI
Red Service
GPP Ship *Lancet*
(Attached GSS *Mercy* pro tem)

www.ingramcontent.com/pod-product-compliance
Lightning Source LLC
Chambersburg PA
CBHW030416310726
48979CB00002B/440
9798880903436